WHENSHEEPCANNOTSLEEP
THE COUNTING BOOK

Satoshi Kitamura

■ • FARRAR STRAUS GIROUX • NEW YORK
SQUARE FISH

Special thanks to Alison Sage for her editorial knitting

SQUARE
FISH

An Imprint of Macmillan

ISBN 978-0-374-48359-3
Library of Congress catalog card number: 86-45000

Originally published in the United States by Farrar Straus Giroux
First Square Fish Edition: August 2012
Square Fish logo designed by Filomena Tuosto
mackids.com

19 21 23 25 24 22 20 18

AR: 2.4 / LEXILE: 450L

One night a sheep called Woolly could not sleep.
"I'll go for a walk," he said, and wandered
off down the meadow.

He chased a butterfly until it flew away
behind a tall green tree.

There on the tree trunk were two ladybirds, fast asleep. "I'm still wide awake," thought Woolly.

"Hoo, hoo, hoo," called the owls.
"Time to go home."

"It's *our* time to come out," said a family of bats,
flittering overhead.

"Apples," said Woolly.
"I knew it was time for something.
 But they are too high up for me."

"Try climbing," said the squirrels.
"Can't," said Woolly.
"There's a ladder," said the squirrels.

They were right.
Woolly put the ladder against the apple tree
and climbed, rung by rung, until he could
reach the sweet, red apples.

It was a lovely calm evening
and Woolly was not a bit sleepy.
Fireflies were dancing in the air . . .

and grasshoppers were singing in the long grass.

Woolly climbed to the top of a hill to look
at the view. Suddenly, flashing lights zipped
across the sky. Woolly was very scared.

He ran as fast as he could to hide
amongst the trees, jumping over red
tulips as he went.

"What a terrible fright," he panted.
"Where am I?" In front of him was a house
with lots of windows.

The front door was open, so he went in.
There were lots of doors, too.

In one of the rooms, he found some
colored pencils. "Good," said Woolly.
"I'll do some drawing."

He was so pleased with his pictures
that he hung them on the wall.

"I'm hungry again," said Woolly.
He went into the kitchen and cooked himself
some nice green peas.

He took them into the dining room.
"I'm late for supper," he thought.

"Now for a bath," said Woolly,
"with lots of bubbles."

Next door was a little bed, with a pair
of pajamas laid neatly on it.
"Stars are out already," thought Woolly.

"Perhaps I'll just lie down . . .
   in case I feel sleepy."

He began to think.

He thought about his mother and his father and
his sisters and brothers and uncles and aunts.
What were they doing? Were they already asleep?
His family and friends went round in his head.
His eyes closed.

Woolly was fast asleep.

INDEX

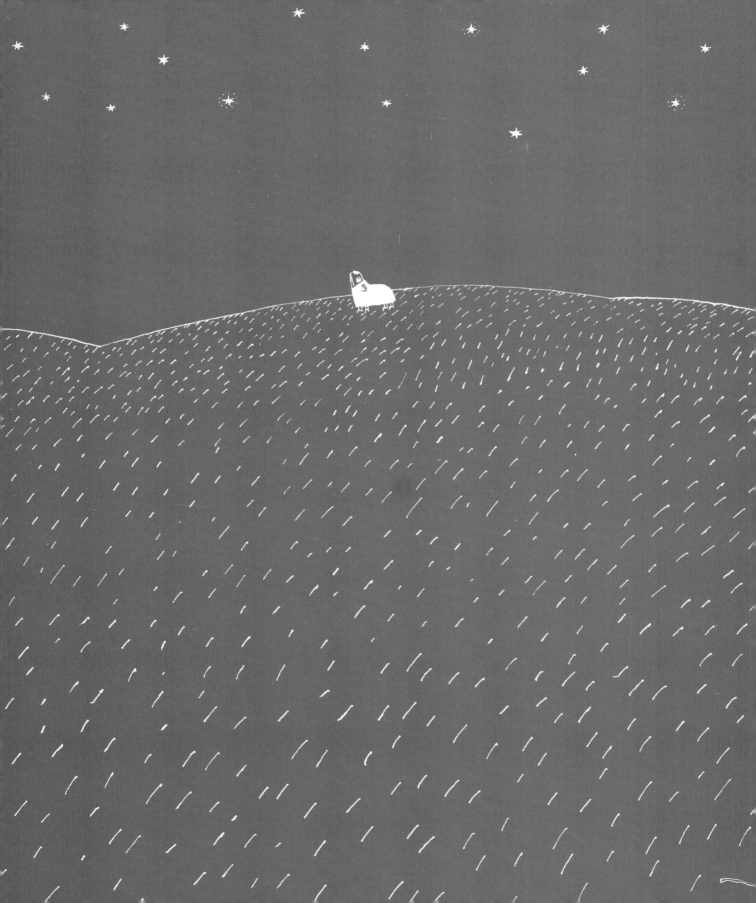

New York Academy of Sciences, Children's Science Book Award
Parents' Choice Award for Illustration

Original and inventive...Satoshi Kitamura has produced a counting book with such elan that it is a joy to look at and a great deal of fun. *—The Horn Book*

Woolly is a truly endearing insomniac. *—Publishers Weekly*

For those who want to put their counting skills to use and enjoy a guessing game along the way. *—Booklist*

SQUARE FISH
AN IMPRINT OF MACMILLAN
175 FIFTH AVENUE, NEW YORK, NY 10010
MACKIDS.COM
PRINTED IN CHINA